amazon
www.angelinahoneybee.com
Other books from
LaTonea Book Publishing
www.latonea.com
Author LaTonea
SILLY KEVIN

The
Christmas
Circus

Angelina Honey Bee explains why we celebrate Christmas. "For to us, a child is born, to us, a son is given; and the government shall be upon his shoulder, and his name shall be called wonderful counselor, mighty God, everlasting father, prince of peace. Glory to God in the highest, and on earth peace among men with whom he is pleased. Thanks be to God for his indescribable gift. Have a Merry Christmas and a Happy Holiday season."

Angelina Honey Bee and her close friends get together for a wonderful Christmas feast that includes a wide variety of delicious dishes, such as turkey, cake, fish, steak, cupcakes, candy, a gingerbread house, and pudding. Everyone sits around the table together. Tiger eats his portion of the best possible food for cats, which happens to be a large piece of fish.

Angelina Honey Bee is surrounded by all of the children, including Tiger the kitten, as they take turns opening their presents after a fun day at the Christmas circus. "Billy, you can change out of your clown outfit now," laughed Angelina Honey Bee. "I think I like it, it truly makes for an interesting conversation starter," says Billy. All the kids laugh.

Angelina Honey Bee gathers all of the children together so that they can choose their gifts for one another. There are a lot of presents under the Christmas tree for everyone to take and enjoy.

On Christmas Day, the kids have a blast going sleigh riding, skiing, and creating funny snowmen in the snow. What's Christmas without all the fun snow activities?

Yippee!

Yippee!

The
Christmas
Circus

Arlo says, "My idea of a perfect holiday gathering looks just like this one right here. To me, the best way to spend Christmas is to have fun with all of my close friends by doing silly fun things together. This will be our new tradition." "I agree 100% Arlo," says Angelina Honey Bee.

The moment has come for a fight with snowballs. What would Christmas be without a spectacular fight of snowballs? The children enjoy themselves by taking turns hurling snowballs at one another as the snow is falling.

Snowball fight!
Snowball fight!

The
Christmas
Circus

The Christmas circus was filled with fun rides and cool circus games where you can win stuffed animals and lots of candy. The day was filled with lots of laughter and smiles from the children. Later they gather together around to take a group picture to remember the day. Candace tells Angelina Honey Bee, "We will definitely have to do it again next year. What a fantastic day."

CLOWN BALLS GAME
The Christmas Circus

There was a gathering of all the children to sing Christmas songs. "There cannot be a Christmas celebration without at least one Christmas carol. Without it, Christmas will never feel quite the same," says Angelina Honey Bee. "Let's begin with the harmony, shall we?" The children each take turns singing and playing their favorite instruments. Sing, sing, sing!

Meow
Meow
Meow

The children enjoy a Christmas-themed circus performance, which includes performances by various animals such as elephants and monkeys. Arlo tells Billy, "I think it is extremely funny that you are dressed up like a clown. You look very entertaining." Angelina Honey Bee tells Billy, "Yeah, that works for you since it fits your personality." Billy remarked, "I'm starting to get into the spirit of the Christmas circus."

The
Christmas
Circus

Everyone has completed their preparations and is now ready with their costumes for this amazing day. The curtain will soon rise on the Christmas circus show. "Oh my, this is definitely not something you see every Christmas," says Angelina Honey Bee. The children are completely fitted up and prepared to go. There is an endless supply of buttery popcorn available and a lot of delicious Christmas cookies. "We can't have cookies without a large glass of milk," says Angelina Honey Bee.

The
Christmas
Circus
MILK

Choo! Choo! Choo! Angelina Honey Bee takes a few of the children on the choo-choo train to the Christmas circus. An alert that sounds like jingle bells are sounded by the train as it approaches the station where it will stop to greet all the other children that are already at the Christmas circus.

It is the morning of Christmas, and Angelina Honey Bee is giving rides on the school bus to some of the children so that they can participate in the festivities taking place today. The children have packed their costumes and are brimming with joy. They cannot contain their excitement at how much fun they are going to have at the Christmas circus today.

CIRCUS
MERRY CHRISTMAS

The children were all hard at work putting the finishing touches on the Christmas circus. As more Christmas decorations are gathered, they will continue to put them across the park. They celebrate by singing and dancing endlessly to the tune of "fa la la la la, fa la la la la." The children are coming very close to completing the process of decorating the Christmas tree and hanging all of the lights. Christmas is tomorrow, so they head home to get some rest before the big celebration.

Angelina Honey Bee and Candace gather a few children to join in to help with putting together the Christmas circus. The kids gather up all the trimmings, ornaments, and lights. "Let's get this Christmas circus in tip-top shape. I can already smell the popcorn and cotton candy. Make sure we have lots of Christmas candy. This is so exciting fa la la, fa la la, everybody," says Arlo.

FUN!
MERRY CHRISTMAS

Angelina Honey and Arlo understand it's going to be a busy day because they are inviting all the kids to the Christmas circus and they need to find volunteers to help get ready for this fantastic celebration. There's far too much to accomplish before the big day. The invitations need to be prepared and sent. The invitations will read, "Dress in your favorite holiday costume and come enjoy the lights, food, music, and fun rides at the Christmas circus."

Come join us at the Christmas circus
Come join us at the Christmas circus

Angelina Honey Bee and Arlo meet with Candace at the park to ask if she would be interested in participating in a Christmas circus. Candace suggests they will need help from friends. "Great idea, Angelina Honey Bee! If we go and get more of our friends involved to put everything together, we will be heroes. There is so much that needs to be done," says Candace.

A few minutes later Angelina Honey Bee knocked at the window of Arlo's bedroom. "This Christmas needs to go down in the history books. There are always gifts, food, and family, which I love, but this Christmas needs to be more exciting and fun," says Arlo. "I have a wonderful suggestion for you. Why not celebrate Christmas by going to a circus that is decked out with gifts, food, costumes, games, music, enjoyable rides, and shows with animals and clowns," says Angelina Honey Bee.

"Wow, it would be an unbelievable experience. Candace needs to be consulted in order for us to formulate a strategy. Let's go meet her at the park," he added quickly.

I ♥ dad
ZZZZ

It began, on a Christmas eve morning when Arlo stood looking out the window of his living room enjoying the fire. "Why does Christmas have to be the exact same boring tradition every single year? It's my favorite holiday, but it's always the same Christmas celebration year after year. I have the desire to make everyone's Christmas more interesting and unforgettable this year. "Let's talk to Angelina Honey Bee and see what she thinks," Arlo sighed.

I'm sure this is the tale of a kid you would all adore. He was so charming and extremely well-loved by everyone. He is an astonishingly clever kid, and the best part about it was that he was unaware of it. He spoke and did smart things, but he never thought to congratulate himself on his cleverness. I don't think he would have had any idea of what I'm about to tell you that will change Christmas for him and all his friends. The whole affair was a little silly, but it was still a memorable experience of what a child dreams of at the Christmas circus.

MERRY
CHRISTMAS

This Book Belongs To

Angelina Honey Bee
What a child dreams of:
The Christmas Circus

For information contact: www.latonea.com or latonea@latonea.com.

Library of Congress Control Number: 2022916466

First Edition September 2022